HOME

CARLETON PLACE
PUBLIC LIBRARY

A house is made of
BOARDS and BEAMS.
A home is made of
LOVE and DREAMS.
— anon.

Dedicated to my
grandparents,
Alice, Betty,
George, and Sid,
for all your
love

tiger tales
an imprint of ME Media, LLC
202 Old Ridgefield Road, Wilton, CT 06897
Published in the United States 2010
Originally published in Great
Britain 2009
by Scholastic Children's Books
a division of Scholastic Ltd.
Text and illustrations copyright
© 2009 Alex T. Smith
CIP data is available
ISBN-13: 978-1-58925-088-8
ISBN-10: 1-58925-088-5
Printed in Singapore
TWP0709

tiger tales

Once there was a house...

a house that was a **home**.
And in the house that was a home
lived four best friends. They were called
One, Two, Three, and Four.

They lived happily
ever after, until . . .

One said, "Let's all move to somewhere different. We could be **pirates** and sail the seven seas!"

The others did **not** think this was a very good idea.

Two said, "I don't want to live on the sea! It's too **wet**. We should all live at the top of a mountain and learn to **yodel**!"

The others didn't think this was a good idea either.

Three sighed and said, "I don't like heights! Let's all live under the ground in a dark, dark cave and collect creepy-crawlies!"

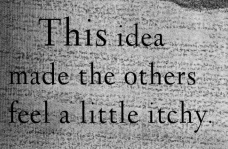

This idea made the others feel a little itchy.

Four had other plans.
"All those ideas are silly!" he said in a very
bossy voice. "We should move to the big city…
and go to parties and boogie-woogie all night long!"

The four friends didn't know what to do.
First they **talked**.

Then they **argued**.

Then they **fought**.

Finally they decided to go their separate ways.

"If I'm going," they all shouted, "I'm taking the house with me!"

One took the door
and stormed off to sea.

Two took the walls and
stomped off up a mountain.

Three took the windows
and scurried to a cave.

TO BIG CITY

Four picked up the floor and
shuffled away to the big city.

All that was left was the roof.

The four not-at-all-best
friends started their new lives
and were very happy...at first.

One became a pirate
and sailed the seas.

But the sea was much bigger and wetter than he had imagined.

And, worst of all, his **house** simply wasn't a **home** when it was just a door.

Two learned how to yodel.

She yodeled and yodeled.
But all she got back was an e c h o.

And she soon realized that her **house** simply wasn't a **home** when it was just four walls.

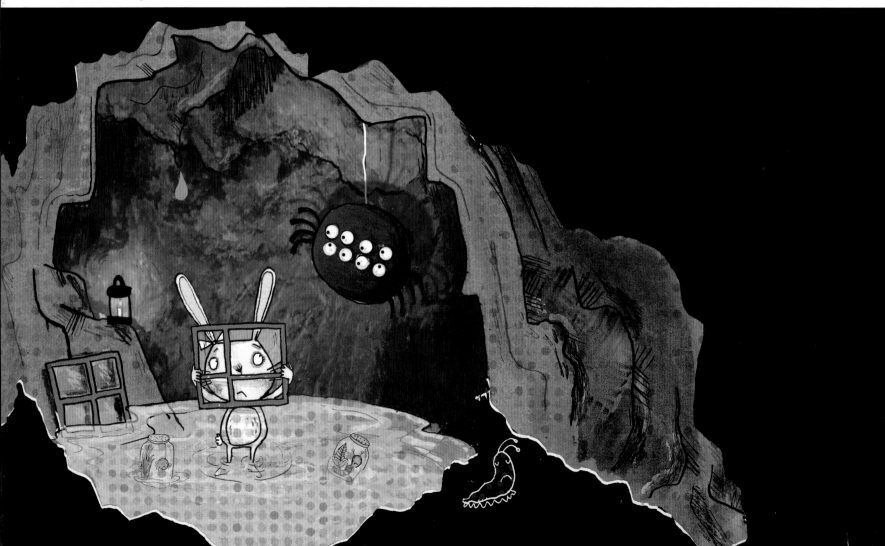

echo

echo

echo

Three collected creepy-crawlies
in her underground cave.

Four went to parties.

But he didn't know anyone and the other guests weren't very friendly.

It was as if they had never seen a badger boogie-woogie before!

And, sure enough, he quickly learned that a house simply wasn't a home when it was just a floor.

All the **not-so-best** friends were sad and lonely.

They missed their **house** that was a **home**.

But most of all, they missed each other.

Something had to be done.

"I'm sorry," said One.

"Me too," said Two.

"Me three," said Three.

"Me four," said Four.

The best-again friends shared a big hug,
and then they began to fix their house…

until it was a home once more.

But they decided to add something new.
Something that meant they could all go to the sea . . .

and they could all learn to yodel on top of a mountain . . .

and they could all collect bugs in the
deepest, darkest caves . . .
and they could all go to the fanciest
parties in the big city.

"Now we can go everywhere together!" they said.

And they did.